September ~~~~

Don

To The

Ke

1001

One
Hundred
Days (Plus One)

For Becky
—M. M.

First Aladdin Paperbacks edition January 2003

Text copyright © 2003 by Simon & Schuster
Illustrations copyright © 2003 by Mike Gordon

ALADDIN PAPERBACKS
An imprint of Simon & Schuster
Children's Publishing Division
1230 Avenue of the Americas
New York, NY 10020

READY-TO-READ is a registered trademark of Simon & Schuster, Inc.

The text for this book was set in CentSchbook BT.
Book design by Sammy Yuen Jr.

Printed in the United States of America
2 4 6 8 10 9 7 5 3 1

Library of Congress Cataloging-in-Publication Data:
McNamara, Margaret.
One hundred days (plus one) / by Margaret McNamara ; illustrated by Mike Gordon.—
1st Aladdin Paperbacks ed.
p. cm. — (Robin Hill School)
Summary: Hannah looks forward to Robin Hill School's celebration of one hundred
days of classes, but when a cold keeps her home the day of the party she decides to
bring in the one hundred buttons she found anyway.
ISBN 0-689-85535-4 (pbk.) — ISBN 0-689-85536-2 (library edition)
[1. Schools—Fiction. 2. Buttons—Fiction. 3. Counting.] I. Gordon, Mike, ill. II. Title.
PZ7.M232518 On 2003
[E]—dc21
2002008834

One Hundred Days (Plus One)

Written by Margaret McNamara
Illustrated by Mike Gordon

Ready-to-Read
Aladdin Paperbacks
New York   London   Toronto   Sydney   Singapore

Hannah was excited.

Only one week to go
until the party
to celebrate
one hundred days in school.

"That is a long time
to be in school,"
said Hannah.

Mrs. Connor told the class,
"Next Friday,
please bring in
100 little things
to share."

Hannah decided
to bring in buttons.

On Monday, Hannah
found 20 white buttons.

On Tuesday she found
57 mixed buttons.

On Wednesday
she found
4 cat buttons,
6 diamond buttons,

and 13 buttons
with no holes.

On Thursday, Hannah counted her buttons from 1 to 100.

CHOOoooo

Then she sneezed.

On Friday,
Hannah had a cold.
"No school for you today,"
said her mother.
"On Monday you will
feel better."

On Monday I will feel
worse, thought Hannah.

The party is today.
And I am not there.

On Monday, Hannah's cold
was gone.

She wore her favorite
sweater to school.
It had one big orange button.

Hannah remembered
the 100 buttons.

She had put them
in her backpack,
even though she had
missed the party.

When the school bell rang,
Mrs. Connor said,
"Today is a special day.
What is one hundred
plus one?"

Hannah knew the answer.
"One hundred and one!"
she said.

"Right!" said Mrs. Connor.

"Today we have been in school
for one hundred and one days."
Hannah's friends were smiling.

They showed
101 grains of rice,

101 hair ribbons,

and 101 postcards.

"I only brought in
100 buttons,"
said Hannah.

"I did not think
to bring in one more,"
she said.

She remembered the button
on her sweater.
"Here is my plus one!"
she said.

"I thought one hundred days
was a long time
to go to school,"
said Hannah.

101
days

"And now I have gone
for one hundred plus one!"